Grandma's Honey Icing

2 cups powdered sugar
2 tablespoons milk
1 tablespoon honey or corn syrup
1 teaspoon vanilla

1. Blend ingredients.

2. Keep mixture stiff to use in a piping bag or add more milk (drop by drop) to thin into a spreadable frosting.

For my sweet sister, Kris,
and, as always, for Sebastian.

Published by Two Lions, New York
www.apub.com

Amazon, the Amazon logo, and Two Lions are trademarks of Amazon.com, Inc., or its affiliates.

ISBN-13: 9781542029223
ISBN-10: 1542029228

The illustrations were rendered in gouache and colored pencil.
Book design by Tanya Ross-Hughes

Printed in China
First Edition

10 9 8 7 6 5 4 3 2 1

The Best Gift for Bear

by Jennifer A. Bell

two lions

Hedgehog had spent the morning decorating cookies
for her friends and neighbors.

She made snowflakes for the mice,
trees for the squirrels,

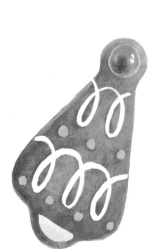

and a special rabbit for each rabbit.
Hedgehog knows a LOT of rabbits.

But she still had one more gift to bake,
and Hedgehog was beginning to worry!

"What do I make for Bear?" she wondered.

She had been thinking of ideas all day.

Ice skates?

Bear had taught her to twirl and glide.

Butterflies?

Bear loved to find them in the meadow.

Sunflowers?

Bear had shown her how tall they grow.

"A few cookies are not enough!" she thought.
"Bear should have a grand gift, a special gift,
something wonderful . . . just like Bear."

Hedgehog was stumped.

When she arrived back home and saw her frosted roof,
Hedgehog had an idea.

She drafted a plan, warmed her oven, . . .

. . . and happily baked her way
into the night.

Flour and eggs.

Sugar and spice.

Roll it. Cut it.

Bake it up nice!

Early the next morning she got to work.

Brick by brick,

swirl by swirl,

Hedgehog built her gift.

It was grand, it was special, it was WONDERFUL . . . just like Bear.

It was also heavy, but Hedgehog pulled it
smoothly across the snow.
She would be at Bear's by nightfall.

But as she made her way along the path,
the wind began to whip around her.
"I'll have to hurry," she thought.

She *pulled* . . .

She *pushed* . . .

Whoosh!!

In an instant her gift became a pile of crumbs.

Grand, special, WONDERFUL Bear!

"What a mess, Bear! I wish you could have
seen your gift before it fell apart."

"I'm just glad you are safe and warm," said Bear.
"You should have seen the mess I made earlier!
I tried to bake you a gift too . . .

". . . but I thought I'd try again tomorrow."

"Let's bake it together!" said Hedgehog.

A day with a friend is the best gift of all!